Mr. Boggarty

The Halloween Grump

Book 1

By Tevin Hansen

Handersen Publishing LLC
Lincoln, Nebraska

Handersen Publishing LLC
Lincoln, Nebraska

Mr. Boggarty: The Halloween Grump
Book 1

Text copyright © 2014 Tevin Hansen
Cover copyright © 2015 Handersen Publishing
Cover Design Handersen Publishing

Manufactured in the United States of America.

ISBN-13: 978-1941429044

Publisher Website: www.handersenpublishing.com
Publisher Email: editors@handersenpublishing.com

For the Rock Man.

(He hated all trick-or-treaters equally.)

Contents

Chapter One
The Halloween Grump

Mr. Boggarty is the mean old man who lives in the big spooky house at the end of Shady Way. His house is old, and ugly, and in need of a paint job and a new roof. There's no fence, no grass, no flowers, and only one tree—a tall ugly tree that looks like a huge skeleton hand reaching down to grab anyone who gets too close.

Kids from the other side of town have heard of him, and even they know it's wise to keep away. And the further away, the better.

As far as the house goes, other than being old and ugly, Mr. Boggarty's mansion is also very *spooky*.

"If I were a ghost," kids would say, "I'd want to live in *that* house."

Most kids think Mr. Boggarty's house should be spelled:

S—P—O—O—K—H—O—U—S—E

Naturally, kids have always assumed that the owner of such a spooky house must be the grumpiest, meanest person who ever lived. Neighborhood kids have nothing to base this on, since no one ever dares to speak to Mr. Boggarty.

"Think of the grumpiest, ugliest, most shriveled up old man you can," some kid might say when asked about Mr. Boggarty. "Got a picture in your mind? Well, Mr. Boggarty is ten times uglier, meaner, and more shriveled up than that."

"What's the meanest thing he's ever done?" some new kid might ask.

To which the reply is always, "What *hasn't* he done! How about not hand out Halloween candy for the last fifteen years! Mr. Boggarty doesn't like kids, and he doesn't like Halloween. He's the Halloween Grump."

Chapter Two
Candy

Every kid believes that all adults should hand out treats on Halloween, even if it's gross stuff like black licorice, or candy corn, or those disgusting Circus Peanuts that taste like Styrofoam. Most kids can't stand these types of gross candy, but it's still better than getting nothing.

Kids may be young, but they are observant enough to know that money can be a touchy subject with parents. But those same kids are candy experts. They will quickly tell you that the pharmacy down the road sells cheap candy for 99¢ a bag, and how grownups need to get their priorities straight when October 31st rolls around.

Trixie Cole, speaker of plain truth, often says, "Kids in America *need* sugar. It's a scientifically proven fact that kids require sugar to survive." Trix usually says things like this while sucking down a 64oz. Slurpee, or seeing who can stuff the most Bubble Tape in their mouth.

"I'm no doctor," Trix would say, "but I do know that kids need sugar for a healthy growing body. We don't need a sugar I.V. or anything. Just five or six servings a day."

All her friends agreed.

"It's like that pyramid with the five food groups they teach us about at school," Trix went on. "Haven't you guys ever noticed that super small pointy part at the top? The part with the word *sugar* written inside it? If grownups knew what they were talking about, they'd change the words around so that sugar was written inside the big box at the bottom."

In the kid world, not handing out candy on Halloween is wrong.

Wrong, wrong, wrong.

Chapter Three
Trixie

If there's one kid who rules the neighborhood, it is definitely Trixie Cole. She's a tough one to explain. She has short blonde hair, a mostly pretty face (when she's not scowling), and she's tougher than most of the neighborhood boys.

Mr. Cole is a professional hockey player. He gets paid to slam other hockey players into the boards and sometimes gets into fights. He is very tough. So is his daughter.

Most kids around the neighborhood know not to mess with Trixie Cole. And if there's one thing kids at school know *not* to call her, it would be to never, ever, ever call her Pretty Princess.

That would be bad.

Jonathan Booth, a fifth grade bully, had to learn this the hard way—the *humiliating* way.

Trix was playing tetherball down on the school playground with her friends one day when Jonathan came looking for trouble. He found it all right. He made the "Pretty Princess" comment, which got a giggle from his friends. The next thing he knew, he found himself knocked to the ground, in pain, and missing a tooth.

"Who's the princess now?" Trix asked, standing over Jonathan, ready to strike again. "Smile, Pretty Princess!"

Trix had knocked out one of Jonathan's front teeth with a solid elbow-to-the-face. If Mr. Cole had done this same thing in a hockey game, he would've been sent to the penalty box for two minutes. Trix got sent home for the rest of the day, which was kind of like a double-bonus instead of a penalty.

But that's not the scary part. The scary part is that all this happened three years ago. Trix was in second grade at the time. No one has messed with her since.

Chapter Four
Frank

Frank's parents aren't cruel, but they *did* name their only child Frank. That's pretty cruel.

Frank's parents are Mr. and Mrs. Dinkins. They are very nice people, but Trix thinks they're complete sickos for giving their only son such a boring, old-fashioned name. It's a name that practically begs to be made fun of with nicknames like Frank-n-Beans, or Frankfurter, or Frankenfarter.

Frank is really smart. He gets straight A's in all his classes. He's a nice kid with very good manners, and he also has a weird disease. It's not really a disease, but sometimes he gets made fun of because he talks backwards. Frank has something called Reverse Speech Syndrome.

If you say, "Hi, Frank. How are you today?" Then Frank might respond with, "Asking for thanks, fine just am I."

Most kids can figure out what he said if it's something easy. But if you get into a conversation with him…watch out.

Frank has some really weird dreams too. He loves to tell people about them. He might say, "Means it think you do what? Me at peanuts throwing and school at playground the around me chasing monkeys wild of pack a about dream weirdest the had I night last. What guess, hey?"

Sometimes he catches himself when he says something backwards, then he turns his words around and says it the right way. Most times he doesn't even notice.

Chapter Five

Darren

Darren is Trix's best friend. They live next door to each other, and they both like lots of the same stuff. They like the same music, the same video games, the same sports, even the same foods—except for sushi. Trix drew the line at sushi. She learned all about it at Darren's birthday dinner last month.

"Ew! What's this nasty stuff?" she asked *very* loudly at a popular Sushi Bar.

"It's sashimi," Darren told her. "Try it. You'll like it."

"*Raw* fish?" Trix had her face all squished up. "I don't even like cooked fish." Instead of trying it, she pigged out on Miso soup and Edamame instead. Then she sat there and watched Darren and his family chow down on eel, octopus, and raw Salmon.

So, other than the whole sushi thing, Trix figures that she and Darren are pretty much exactly alike.

Here's the catch: Trix claims that Darren is the one who always gets *her* into trouble. Darren claims it's the other way around.

Trix has often said, "I wouldn't trade Darren for anyone else in the whole world . . . most days."

Chapter Six

Darby

Darby is from Australia. He has a unique accent, which makes him popular just for that. He's always saying funny things like, "Naw, mate—that sounds like some bloody hard yakka!" or "Sure, mate! Sounds like the dinky-di!"

Darby gets into trouble sometimes for the things he says. Like last week when he asked the teacher a question in Aussie-speak.

"Yes, Darby?" asked their teacher, Miss Shields. "Do you have a question?"

"Naw, Sheila. Jus' need a trip to the dunny, ya know? Gotta take care of some shonky business. Ya deeg?"

Mrs. Shields thought he said something really bad. But all he said was that he needed to use the bathroom.

Darby came to their school halfway through third grade. His folks split up back in Australia, so he and his mom moved to America, where she married an American bloke.

Trix and her friends liked Darby right away. They all liked the way he talked and how he always made them laugh with all the funny things he said.

Girls liked him because they thought he was cute.

Boys liked him because he owned a dirt bike.

Chapter Seven
Preston

Preston is tough. But he's not as tough as Trix. He is definitely the biggest daredevil at school. Even the sixth graders can't compete with him.

Preston is always coming up with crazy things to do. Just last week someone dared him to walk along the railing in front of the school. It was pretty impressive considering that the railing is over a hundred feet long. The bad part was that he got caught because the railing was right outside the school's main office. The Principal was in his office doing paperwork when he looked outside and saw a student walking past his window.

Another time, Preston climbed up onto the roof of his house so he could jump onto a tree branch ten feet away. He landed perfectly on the branch, but then the branch snapped in half and he fell.

Preston broke his wrist on the landing.

But some good came of it. Because of his cast, he got all kinds of special treatment from his parents—stuff like watching movies, extra ice cream at dinner time, and he got out helping with the household chores. Plus he didn't have to do homework for six weeks because the cast was on his right arm, what he claimed was his homework arm.

Trix got grounded for a whole month because of that stunt. Her mom found out that *she* was the one who dared him to do it.

Chapter Eight
Halloween Around The World

In Mexico, kids celebrate Day of the Dead instead of Halloween. It sounds really bad, but it's not. It's a wonderful celebration with lots of candy and fireworks.

Frank's family knows all about Halloween in Mexico because they flew down there two years ago for a church mission trip. When they came back, Frank had a million stories to tell.

"People love Halloween down in Mexico!" Frank told them when he got back. They thought the trip had miraculously fixed his Reverse Speech Syndrome. Then Frank said, "Stuff fun of kinds all and parade big a have and candy homemade make and fireworks off shoot they, treating-or-trick going of instead!"

In Austria, people leave bread and something to drink on the kitchen table on the night of Halloween. They do this just in case any souls that have departed the earth come back and get hungry.

In China, people do the same kind of thing. Only instead of bread, they put a bowl of noodles in front of family pictures. Then they light a candle so their departed family members can see in the dark and don't get lost on their way home.

In Australia, where Darby's from, people don't celebrate Halloween at all. Darby had to explain to everyone that people in Australia celebrate some famous guy who died hundreds of years ago.

"Back in Oz, us keeds don't have Halloween like you blokes," Darby told them. "Instead, we celebrate Guy Fawkes!"

"Guy Farts?" Trix asked.

"*Fawkes*, mate," Darby corrected her. "Guy Fawkes, keeper of the gunpowder! Ya see, way back when, in sixteen-oh-five, I reckon, old Fawkes-y come a guster when those pollys came to have a Captain Cook, ya deeg?"

Someone would usually say, "Sure, Darby, we deeg," even though they had no idea what he was talking about.

Darby was always going on and on about Oz, which is a nickname for Australia. They all had to admit that the place sounded really cool *and* kind of scary. First off, it's an island where all the criminals were sent to live, so it's kind of like a humongous Alcatraz prison. But they have lots of cool stuff in Australia: great white sharks, stingrays, and giant jelly fish that can paralyze every muscle in your body.

"Australia sounds pretty neat," Trix told him. "But no Halloween? That's just not right."

In America, people hand out candy. If you *don't*…then prepare for retaliation.

Chapter Nine
Eggs

It all started one day at the end of summer vacation. That's when Trix, who was already thinking months ahead, came up with a brilliant idea for a Halloween prank.

Out of the blue, Trix said, "Why don't we egg Mr. Boggarty's house this year for Halloween? That mean old geezer *never* hands out candy on Halloween. He hates kids, and he hates Halloween. His house deserves to get splattered with rotten eggs."

Every kid knows that if you're planning on egging somebody's house, the best thing to use is a rotten egg. And not just one or two rotten eggs. You need lots of them. Cartons of them.

The very same day that Trix came up with her brilliant idea, each of them went home and took a full carton of eggs from the fridge. Everybody's mom asked the same thing: "Honey, have you seen the carton of eggs I just bought?" The standard reply was, "Nope. Sorry, mom! I have no idea what you're talking about!"

They hid five cartons of eggs in the woods just down the road from Trix's house. And to get the eggs extra rotten they poked a pin-sized hole in the top of each egg, allowing air to get in and rot the insides.

That was back in August. By the time October rolled around, the eggs were completely rancid. They had rotted to a pukey, putrid perfection.

Preston let them test one on him.

"Do it, Darby! Throw it!"

"Alright, mate. Simmer down," Darby said. "Let me get me good arm on, aw'right?"

It was Trix's idea to test one out. And since Darby was the best at baseball, he got to throw the egg. He launched the putrid projectile as hard as he could right at Preston. The rotten egg exploded all over Preston's shirt, splattering in his face, in his hair, even on his neck and shoulder. Somehow a huge chunk even got lodged in his ear. The smell was so bad that Preston had to take off his shirt during the walk home. The putrid aroma was burning everyone's nostrils.

"I think the eggs are ready," Trix said, pulling her own shirt up over her nose.

Then Darby came up with the best dare of all. He dared Preston to *eat* one of the eggs.

It was the first time that Preston chickened out on a dare. No one held it against him though. Those eggs were practically radioactive.

Chapter Ten
Costumes

Frank's mom is a seamstress. This Halloween she did a great job with his costume. Frank looked just like a mutant ninja turtle, right down to his cool green mask.

It was a great improvement over last year's costume, which cost him a trip to the dentist because of a chipped tooth.

Last Halloween, Frank went as his favorite chess piece, a Rook. The costume looked great, even had a built in candy bag attached to the front. But there were no arm holes in his costume. So on Halloween night, at the very first house they ran up to, Frank made it up the stairs just fine, but then he took a bad fall on the way down. He ended up with a chipped tooth and a really cool black eye, all purple and yellow.

Preston decided to go as the world's most infamous green monster, *Frankenstein*. Unfortunately, Preston's mom wasn't any good at sewing. He was dressed entirely in green, right down to his socks. The only problem was that nobody knew who he was supposed to be.

"The Jolly Green Giant?" Preston guessed.

"The Incredible Hulk?" Darren suggested.

Fed up, Preston shouted, "FRANKENSTEIN!"

Trix said, "Oh. I thought you were dressed up like a giant booger."

Preston chose Frankenstein because he was forced to read the book for summer school—the graphic novel, anyway. The weirdest part was that he actually enjoyed it. Now he was slowly reading his way through the *real* book, which is ever scarier.

Darren went as his favorite movie character, Captain Jack Sparrow. He looked just like the guy from the movies. If you closed your eyes and ignored the fact that he sounded like a twelve year old pirate, you'd think you were talking to the real Captain Jack.

Their teacher, Mrs. Shields, loved those movies too. She thought it was the funniest thing when Darren answered her questions in class yesterday using his Captain Jack voice. But his act got old really quick. He'd been doing it all day at school, annoying everyone he encountered with a barrage of movie quotes. By lunchtime Trix wanted to poke him right in the eye—the one without a patch.

So she did.

Darby's costume was by far the most bizarre. He made it himself. And by the looks of it, he worked really hard to get everything just right.

His costume consisted of a long skinny cardboard box, all painted up silver, which he then crawled into and wore like a jacket. Several empty paper towel rolls were stuck to the top of his head, representing the handle. His face was painted up like an on/off switch.

"Give up? I'm a Vac!" Darby said when everyone was out of guesses.

Everyone looked at him funny. "A what?"

"I'm a vacuum cleaner, mate! See? Listen 'ere!" Darby even tape-recorded his Mom vacuuming the house so he could have sound effects. "Oy! Authentic sound, mate!" Darby pressed the stop button on his tape-recorder. "Well? What'cha think? How'd I do for me first homemade Halloween costume?"

"Great, Darby," Trix said. "Really…different."

Having been in the U.S.A. for only a couple years, Darby hadn't quite gotten the hang of Halloween.

Everyone gave him full credit for originality.

Trix's costume idea came from her favorite book, a wonderful adventure story written by L. Frank Baum. Unlike Preston, she had always enjoyed reading. And if anyone ever gave her grief about it, she punched them.

The book was called *The Wizard of Oz*.

"That movie was made back in the eighteen hundreds," Preston told her. "It was the first movie ever made! Back when movie cameras were first invented. I read that somewhere, I think . . ."

Darren, Preston, Frank, and Darby had to force themselves not to laugh when Trix came out the front door wearing her Halloween costume. She was dressed up like Dorothy. She looked very cute in her blue dress, pigtails, and bright red shoes. It was just weird to see her dressed like that. None of them had ever seen her wear a dress before. Normally, she wore ripped jeans, T-shirts, and worn out sneakers.

"What?" Trix said, eyeing them suspiciously. "Why are you guys laughing?"

"We're not laughing."

One of them accidently let out a snort.

Trix cracked her knuckles.

Chapter Eleven
October 31st

By 4:30 p.m. Trix and her friends were all set to pull off the greatest Halloween prank ever—or at least the best prank this year.

Everyone was sitting on the steps outside Trix's house, in costume, waiting for the sun to go down. The unwritten rule of Halloween night is that big kids can't start trick-or-treating until it's *completely* dark outside. Little kids can start early, though.

Frank said, "Treating-or-trick start can we so outside dark get and up hurry would it wish I."

"Me too, mate," Darby said. "Can't wait to get a nibble on. Especially some of that yummy choc!"

It wasn't quite dark yet, but the neighborhood was already alive with kids running around and acting like lunatics. Some older neighborhood kids were already lighting off firecrackers and bottle rockets.

Out of boredom, Trix dared Preston to ring someone's doorbell and scream, "Trick or treat!" as loud as he could.

As usual, Preston did it in two seconds. Too bad for him that he picked Mrs. Whickerby's house. When he screamed "TRICK OR TREAT!!" right in Mrs. Whickerby's face the moment she opened the front door, she freaked out. The poor old woman was so startled that she whacked Preston over the head with the dust pan she was holding. Then she chased him all over the front yard with it.

Everyone watched this happen from the other side of the road, laughing until their sides hurt.

Chapter Twelve
Into The House

By five p.m. Trix and the others were crouched behind the big ugly tree in Mr. Boggarty's front yard. It was completely dark outside by now, so they were all safe from sight, hidden from any nosy onlookers.

No one would catch them because nobody ever bothered walking down to the end of Shady Way, where Mr. Boggarty lived, alone, in his big spooky mansion. There were no street lights nearby, so no one would notice them launching five cartons of rotten eggs at his house.

"You guys ready?" Trix asked.

"Um…"

"You sound nervous, Darren?" Trix said. "You sure you aren't too chicken to do this?"

Darren tried to answer in his Captain Jack voice, but nothing came out. He *was* scared, but he wasn't letting on.

They'd all pulled Halloween pranks before, but nothing like this. And never on anyone so mean. On the off chance that they got caught, there was no telling what Mr. Boggarty might do.

Darren suddenly unsheathed his jeweled plastic sword and shouted, "Down with the old bugger, matey!" Then he raced across Mr. Boggarty's front yard and up the porch steps.

The others watched him inch his way along the porch, slowly creeping his way towards the front door. The plan was to ding-dong-ditch Mr. Boggarty's house to make sure he wasn't home before blasting the outside with stinky rotten eggs.

Darren reached the window closest to the front door. The curtains were closed, so nothing could be seen inside.

Then he stopped.

That was as far as he could go. His legs had stopped working. He had suddenly become paralyzed by fear.

"What's he doing?" Preston whispered.

"Dunno, mate," Darby said. "Havin' second thoughts, by the looks of it."

Finally, after watching Darren for about a minute, they realized he wasn't going any further. Not without help.

"C'mon," Trix said. "He's going to ruin it for all of us."

With Trix in the lead, the rest of them raced across the lawn, keeping low to the ground, joining their frozen friend on the porch. He looked like a mime, not a fearless pirate.

"Welly, well, well? What's this, I see? It's me first mates!" Captain Darren said, trying to act as if everything was under control. "This be a soirée for one, matey! I've got things under control, savvy?"

"Darren?" Trix whispered. "Drop the accent, okay? Otherwise I'm going to have to hurt you."

"Sorry," Darren said in his normal voice. He whispered, "I wasn't scared until I got up here. Now my legs won't move!"

"Yeah, we noticed," Trix said. She began pushing him towards the front door.

"Hey!" Darren hissed. "Quit shoving me, *Dorothy*. I'll go when I'm good and ready!"

"We don't have all night," Trix said. "If somebody doesn't take charge, we'll never get it done. So get moving, *Captain*."

Darren continued to make up excuses about chickening out, so Trix shoved him out of the way and headed straight for the front door.

She tried the doorknob.

C-R-R-R-E-E-E-A-A-A-A-K!

The door opened.

Chapter Thirteen
The Prank

Light from the living room spilled out onto the front porch. There were no sounds coming from inside the house, so that was a good sign. From where they stood, it looked like the coast was clear.

Trix was ready. But one thing still bothered her.

"You guys?" Trix asked. "Why is the living room light still on?" It was the first time she could ever remember seeing a light on *inside* Mr. Boggarty's house on Halloween night. His house was always completely dark long before trick-or-treaters started parading the streets.

Trix cautiously poked her head inside.

"What do you see?" Darren asked. "What's in there? Is it one big torture chamber?"

Darren squealed like a piglet when Trix grabbed him by the wrist and yanked him inside. He slapped his free hand over his face, hoping to shield his eyes from the horrors within.

Trix was not impressed.

"This place isn't scary," Trix said. "Looks like the most boring guy on the planet lives here." She expected to see bugs crawling on the floor, or maybe giant spider webs stretching across the ceiling. She imagined dozens of creepy taxidermy animal heads nailed to the walls, or paintings of demons and other scary stuff hanging everywhere. Mutilated sculptures! Blood-splattered walls!

Not kitsch.

There was a dusty old area rug spread out on the living room floor, and all sorts of antique furniture that looked like it hadn't been sat on in years. The floors were all hardwood, and the walls were done up with decorative trim. There were lots of pictures hanging on the walls, but nothing morbid. There was even one painting of a cartoony-looking guy standing on a bridge, holding his face and letting out a Scream.

"Get in here, you guys," Trix said, poking her head back out the front door. The other three were still on the porch, huddled together, too scared to enter.

"C'mon, you chickens," Trix said. "It's safe. There's nobody here but us."

Because Trix seemed so confident that nobody was home, they decided it must be safe to enter Mr. Boggarty's house.

Darren was busy exploring when suddenly he stopped. He was the first one to notice it.

"Trix?" Darren asked. "Why is there a jack-o-lantern on the table?"

It was true.

There *was* a pumpkin on the table. It had a silly face carved into it. Two elongated eyes and a big pumpkin-y smile. There was a candle flickering inside.

"That's weird," Trix said. "I wonder why there's a—"

Before Trix could even finish her sentence, the others toppled over each other, falling onto the living room floor in a big heap. They'd been trying to see inside without actually stepping into Mr. Boggarty's house. Then they all lost their balance.

"We did it, mates!" Darren said in his pirate voice. "We besieged ol' Boggarty's cabin without so much as a wink of trouble!" Now that he realized Mr. Boggarty's house was empty, his courage had magically returned.

"*Shhh!*" Trix hissed. "Be quiet, Captain Bigmouth! Something's wrong."

They waited a while.

They listened a while longer.

When nothing happened, Trix shrugged off her uneasy feeling. Then, with a big grin on her face, she produced her carton of rotten eggs. The others did the same.

"Change of plan, guys," Trix announced. "We're going to egg the *inside* of Mr. Boggarty's house. The place will smell bad for weeks!"

Five cartons of rotten eggs were ready to fly.

"Ready..." Trix said.

"Aim..." Preston said.

Everyone had an egg in their hand, ready to launch. They were finally going to get Mr. Boggarty back for all these years of never handing out candy.

"We need to hurry up," Frank whispered. "Something or warthogs into all us turn he'll or house his egging us catching and home coming Boggarty Mr. want don't we."

Before Frank could spit out another backwards sentence...

The door slammed shut.

And then . . .

THE
        LIGHTS
                WENT
                        OUT.

Chapter Fourteen
The Ghost

"Where *are* you guys?" Trix had her hands out in front of her, searching for her friends in the dark. "I can't see a thing!"

"Over here!" someone said.

"Over here *where?*" Trix asked.

It was so dark that no one knew what was happening. Everyone was bumping into each other, falling down, and crashing into tables and chairs.

"Preston, is that you?" Trix asked, then she grabbed someone's box-shaped arm.

"Steady, mate!" Darby yelped. "You're messin' up me costume!"

"Sorry, Darby," Trix said. "If you hadn't noticed, it's kind of hard to see right now."

There wasn't even a smidge of light peeking in through the windows. Not from a streetlight, car headlight, or neighborhood mom or dad carrying a flashlight.

The house was like a giant shadow.

Nervous voices filled the darkness.

"What's going on?"

"What's happening?"

"Here of out get can we so door the find *please* somebody will!"

Five frightened kids fumbled around in the dark, not knowing what was going on. All sorts of horrible scenarios played out in their minds, thinking about what was going to happen if they didn't find a way out soon.

Someone screamed.

Panic set in when a ghostly green light appeared at the end of the hallway. Everyone noticed it at the exact same time. Being so dark, it was kind of hard to miss.

A huge, green light was coming down the hall towards them. There was something else in the house with them . . .

A bright green ghost came flying into the room! It floated all around the living room, spinning in circles, and making horrific ghostly noises.

"Get outta here!" Frank shouted at the ghost. "From came you dimension evil whatever to back go!"

This wasn't some actor on TV pretending to be a ghost, or some kind of computer generated graphic. This was a *real* ghost!

"Leave us alone!" Trix yelled.

"Oy, mate! We'es just keeds!" Darby shouted. "We're not stealing anything! We're just here to toss a few rotten cackleberries!"

"Be quiet, Darby!" Trix hissed. "Don't *tell* him!"

There was nothing they could do. Nowhere to run. They were trapped inside a spooky old house with a glowing green ghost.

Frank couldn't help himself. "Um, Mr. Ghost, sir? You are brains our eat to going not you're?"

"*WHAT DID YOU SAY?!*" screeched the ghost. Its voice was distorted and awful. "SONNY, I DIDN'T UNDERSTAND A WORD YOU JUST SAID!"

"Don't yell at him!" Trix snapped. "He has Reverse Speech Syndrome, you dumb ghost!" Trix couldn't believe she'd just insulted an apparition.

"OH. SORRY," the ghost said. "I DIDN'T MEAN TO MAKE FUN OF YOUR STRANGE TALKING DISORDER. I USED TO STUTTER MYSELF, BACK WHEN I WAS JUST A YOUNGIN' LIKE YOU. I MEAN, BACK WHEN I WAS JUST A YOUNG GHOST…"

An uncomfortable silence filled the dark living room.

"Sorry, Mr. Ghost," Preston said. "My friend just wants to know if you're going to eat our brains. Lately he's had this weird fascination with brain-munching zombies. It's because he snuck downstairs one night after his mom and dad went to sleep so he could watch a super scary movie. He's all traumatized now."

"NO, I'M NOT GOING TO EAT YOUR BRAIN, NITWIT! I'M A GHOST, NOT A ZOMBIE!"

The ghost started flying around the living room in circles again, going, "OOOH! AHH! BOOGA-BOOGA-BOOGA!"

All of a sudden—

Thunk.

Trix was pretty sure that the ghost crashed into the coffee table. It sounded like it hurt. The ghost said something that sounded very much like, "Ow."

"Did you just say *ow*?" Trix asked the ghost.

"NO, I DID NOT SAY *OW*," the ghost roared. "I SAID, UH...*NOW*... AS IN NOW I'VE GOT YOU!"

The ghost started doing his ooga-booga thing all over again. It wasn't nearly as scary the second time around.

When the bright green ghost was finished, he yelled at them to sit down.

"ON YOUR KEISTERS! ALL OF YOU!" the ghost demanded. They all did as they were told.

Trix was lucky because she was able to feel her way to the nice comfy sofa she'd been standing close to when the lights went out. The others had to sit on the floor—except for Darby, who found a chair to sit in. But he accidently broke his vacuum costume in half when he tried to sit down.

"Darby, you nong!" he yelled at himself. "Ya just busted up yer costume, mate! All that hard work for nuthin'!"

"PIPE DOWN!" screeched the ghost. "THAT MEANS *BE QUIET* FOR THOSE OF YOU UNFAMILIAR WITH THE TERM."

Everyone piped down.

Then the ghost informed them that he was going to tell them all a story.

A ghost story.

Chapter Fifteen
Souls for Sale

"YOU KIDS SURE PICKED THE WRONG NIGHT TO ENTER *THIS* HOUSE," said the ghost. "OR SHOULD I SAY THE HOUSE OF THE *RECENTLY DEPARTED* MR. BOGGARTY."

The ghost's voice was low and hideous. Kind of like how Darth Vader would sound if he had a terrible sore throat. The voice was not human.

"Recently departed?" Preston asked, somewhere in the dark room. "What does that mean?"

"I MEAN I ROBBED HIS LIFE-FORCE, DUNDERHEAD! I ENTERED THIS HUMBLE ABODE JUST A FEW MINUTES BEFORE YOU FIVE BRATS GOT HERE. I CAUGHT

THAT OLD BUZZARD WHILE HE WAS HAVING A CAT NAP! CAME RIGHT IN AND PLUNDERED HIS CRUSTY OLD SPIRIT."

"You mean took his *soul?*" Trix asked with a shaky voice. She felt very attached to her soul. She couldn't imagine anyone stealing it.

"THAT'S EXACTLY WHAT I DID! I TOOK HIS VERY SOUL! WHAT DO YA THINK OF THAT, MISSY?"

"While he was *sleeping?*" Trix snapped, practically biting the ghost's head off.

"YOU BETCHA!"

Trix let the ghost have it. "Listen here you ugly ghost. You can't just go around breaking into old people's houses and stealing their souls. That's rude!"

"SURE I CAN! I'M A GHOST! I CAN DO WHATEVER I DARN WELL PLEASE, *TRIXIE COLE.*"

Trix sucked in a huge gulp of air at the sound of her name. The ghost knew her *full* name. This was not good.

"AH," said the ghost, floating slowly around the living room. "I'VE GOT YOUR FULL ATTENTION NOW, DON'T I, YOUNG LADY?"

Trix said nothing. She was too scared to talk.

"HERE WE ARE ON HALLOWEEN NIGHT, THE SPOOKIEST NIGHT OF THE YEAR. A TIME FOR TREATS! A TIME FOR TRICKS! A TIME FOR...PRANKS? LIKE MAYBE BREAKING INTO SOMEONE'S HOUSE AND TOSSING A FEW ROTTEN EGGS?"

Now they were all good and scared. Every one of them wondered how in the world the ghost knew all this stuff?

Someone whimpered in the darkness.

"Oh, stop trying to scare us," Trix said, trying to sound brave even though she didn't feel very brave right now. "These guys might be scared of

47

you, but I'm not. So there." She stuck her tongue out at the ghost.

The ghost laughed its horrible laugh. "I PROMISE YOU, *DOROTHY*, THAT BY THE END OF THIS NIGHT YOU WILL BE MORE SCARED THAN YOU'VE EVER BEEN IN YOUR ENTIRE LIFE."

Trix kept quiet.

"YOU SHOULD *ALL* BE SCARED BECAUSE I'M THE ONE WHO PUT THE *FOR SALE* SIGN ON ALL OF YOUR SOULS!"

"Say what, mate?" Darby said. "Me soul's not for sale."

"WELL, THAT'S TOO BAD," the ghost said, "BECAUSE I PUT 'EM UP FOR GRABS ON THE BLACK MARKET. THEY SHOULD SELL PRETTY QUICK, I IMAGINE. KID SOULS ARE BIG BUSINESS THESE DAYS. YOUR LITTLE SOULS ARE BOUND TO GET MORE THAN FAIR MARKET VALUE. THE FIVE

DEMONS WILL PURCHASE YOUR PINT-SIZED SOULS IN A HEARTBEAT."

"The Five Demons?" Trix asked nervously. "Who are they? And for that matter, who are *you?*"

"WHO AM I? WHO AM *I?*" roared the ghost. "I'LL TELL YOU WHO I AM, MISSY. I JUST SO HAPPEN TO BE…"

Everyone had to wait silently in the dark.

"I AM—HOLD ON A SEC…"

After another pause, followed by a clicking sound, scary Halloween music began to play. It began slowly, but soon filled the living room with the sounds of a spooky symphony.

"I AM THE LIME GREEN GHOST OF LINCOLN COUNTY!"

Chapter Sixteen
Dust for Breakfast?

After the ghost's dramatic introduction, someone hit the floor with a *thud*.

It was Preston. He fainted.

The scary music stopped. Then the Lime Green Ghost of Lincoln County flew across the room. There was shuffling, and movement, and then the sound of splashing water.

The next thing everyone heard was Preston saying, "Yes, Miss Shields? Could you repeat the question please?" Preston didn't know where he was. He thought he'd fallen asleep during class again.

"ALL BETTER NOW?" the ghost asked. "YOU GAVE ME A BIT OF A FRIGHT, THERE, YOUNG FELLA. *HA!* IMAGINE A

TOUGH LITTLE SPUD LIKE YOU FAINTING AT THE MERE SIGHT OF A GHOST."

"Sorry, Mr. Ghost sir," Preston said. "Sometimes I get overwhelmed. It's a medical condition I have. Doctors don't know what it is."

"Yeah, it's called chicken guts," Trix mumbled under her breath, but still loud enough for everyone to hear. But still, Trix knew it was bad news when Preston, the *second* toughest kid in their group of friends, was so scared that he fainted.

"IS THAT RIGHT?" said the ghost. "WELL, SHOW SOME COURAGE NEXT TIME, WILL YA? GEESH! KIDS NOWADAYS ARE NOTHING BUT A BUNCH OF COWARDS. EXCEPT FOR THE YOUNG MISS, I SUPPOSE. SEEMS LIKE SHE'S GOT A BACKBONE."

"True not that's!" Frank suddenly shouted. "Either, coward a not I'm!" Correcting himself, he said, "I mean, I'm not a coward either."

"ALL RIGHT, ALL RIGHT," the ghost said irritably. "SO YOU'RE NOT A COWARD, EITHER. DROP IT ALREADY! BY THE WAY…REMIND ME LATER, BEFORE THE FIVE DEMONS GET HERE, I MEAN…MY SISTER IS A SPEECH THERAPIST. SHE CAN PROBABLY HELP WITH THAT WEIRD SENTENCE REVERSAL THING OF YOURS."

Ghosts being nice? Trix didn't know what to think. None of them did.

"OKAY, LET'S GET THIS SHOW ON THE ROAD, SHALL WE?" said the ghost. "I HAVEN'T GOT ALL NIGHT. BELIEVE IT OR NOT, US GHOSTS HAVE A LIFE TOO!"

"Get what show on the road, Mr. Ghost sir?" Preston asked, still unsure about how to properly address the ghost.

"I'll GLADLY TELL YOU, MR. PRESTON PHILLIPS. BUT ONLY IF YOU CAN CONTROL THAT FLAPPING TONGUE OF YOURS AND STOP INTERRUPTING ME!"

"Sorry."

"YOU JUST DID IT AGAIN!"

"Sorry."

The Lime Green Ghost let out a huge sigh. When the room was quiet enough to his liking, the ghost began to speak.

"ARE THEY STILL TEACHING YOU KIDS ABOUT AMERICAN HISTORY IN SCHOOL? DO ANY OF YOU KNUCKLEHEADS KNOW WHAT THE GREAT DEPRESSION WAS?"

Darren raised his arm in the dark just like he would in class. He felt kind of dumb because it was too dark for anyone to see him waving his hand in the air.

But the ghost saw.

"YES, MR. CLUTTERBAUM?"

The hairs on the back of Darren's neck stood up. Not only did the ghost know *his* full name too, but he also pronounced it correctly. Darren always gets mad when people mispronounce his last name. "It's Clutter*bomb*," he tells people. "Not Clutter*bum*."

"I know what the Great Depression was, Mr. Ghost," Darren said, accidently letting out a high-pitched squawk at the end. His voice was changing, so sometimes he sounded like the air being slowly released from a balloon.

"WELL? WHAT IS IT, SQUEAKY?"

"It happened a long time ago," Darren explained. "Back when the Stock Market crashed."

The ghost said, "SWOOSH! TWO POINTS FOR CLUTTERBAUM!"

Trix thought how weird it was hearing a ghost say a word like "swoosh" as if it knew about basketball.

"Ooh! Ooh!" Preston was waving his hand in the air just like Darren did a moment ago.

"YES, MR. PRESTON WILLOBY? FEELING BETTER NOW? AND WILL YOU PLEASE STOP WAVING YOUR HAND AROUND LIKE A LUNATIC. I CAN SEE YOU JUST FINE."

"I know all about the Great Depression," Preston said. "We learned about it in school last year. It happened back in the nineteen thirties. It's when the whole country got poor and everybody had to eat bowls of dust."

"NO, YOU NINCOMPOOP!" wailed the ghost. "PEOPLE DIDN'T *EAT* THE DUST! GREAT GUSTS OF WIND SWEPT THROUGH THE MIDWEST AND PEOPLE LIVED *IN* THE DUST BOWL. IT'S A FIGURE OF SPEECH, NOODLEHEAD!"

"Oh. Our teacher must've taught us wrong then."

Trix was pretty sure the ghost was shaking its glowing green head at Preston. She heard the ghost mumbling under its breath.

"BUNCH OF NOODLEHEADS," said the ghost. "TOO MUCH TV, NOT ENOUGH BOOKS…"

Chapter Seventeen
The Old Days

The Lime Green Ghost talked up a storm. Sometimes his train of thought wandered off a bit, but mostly he stayed on track.

At one point, Frank started in with the whole brain-eating thing again. "Mr. Ghost, sir?"

"WHAT NOW?"

"Are you *sure* you're not going to eat our brains?" Frank asked. "Positive?"

"OH, BROTHER. WILL YOU KNOCK IT OFF!" said the ghost. "FOR THE LAST TIME, NO, I AM NOT GOING TO EAT YOUR BRAIN! BUT IF YOU KEEP ASKING ME ABOUT IT, THEN MAYBE I WILL COME OVER THERE AND TAKE A NIBBLE OUT OF THAT WET NOODLE YOU CALL A BRAIN!"

Frank sobbed pitifully in the dark.

"Simmer down, mate," Darby said, trying to calm his friend down. "He ain't going to eat your brains, bud. Ghosts eat, um…they eat vegemite!"

"YES. THAT'S WHAT WE GHOSTS EAT. VE-GI-UHH, VEGI-SOMETHING…"

"*Mite*, mate," said Darby. "Vegemite."

"WHATEVER!" wailed the ghost. He was just thankful for the help in trying to get Frank to stop whining.

"Everything'll be fine, mate," Darby said. Quietly, he added, "I hope…?" Darby is usually pretty calm during crazy situations. He doesn't believe in ghosts or werewolves or vampires. He just believes in something called *Bunyip*, which is a monster that lives in the backwoods of Australia.

"SO YOU'RE THE ONE CALLED DARBY?"

"Sure, mate. I mean ghost-mate."

"FROM NEW ZEALAND, RIGHT?"

"Naw, mate. Oz! Ya know? Aussie."

"UH…"

"Australia, mate!"

"OH. OKAY. GOTCHA…*MATE*," the ghost said. "WHERE WAS I?" asked the ghost. "WE NEED TO GET BACK TO BUSINESS, HERE. NO MORE FOOLIN' AROUND! NOW, SERIOUSLY—WHAT WAS I TALKING ABOUT BEFORE?"

"Well, before you started insulting my friends," Trix said, "you were telling us about the Great Depression."

"AH, YES," the ghost said, clearing its throat. "BACK IN THOSE DAYS KIDS DIDN'T GO DOOR TO DOOR COLLECTING CANDY ON HALLOWEEN NIGHT. BELIEVE IT OR NOT, THERE WAS SUCH A TIME WHEN THERE WAS NO SUCH THING AS THE INTERNET, OR PLAYING VIDEO GAMES ON A FIFTY-TWO INCH HDTV.

BACK THEN IT WAS A TWENTY MINUTE WALK TO THE NEAREST NEIGHBOR. BUT ALL IN ALL, THINGS WERE JUST HUNKY DORY FOR A WHILE. THEN THE GREAT

DEPRESSION CAME ALONG AND KNOCKED HALF THE COUNTY ON THEIR BACKSIDES. IT WAS A TERRIBLE TIME IN THIS COUNTRY'S HISTORY. AND IT'S HERE THAT MY STORY—AND YOUR *DEMISE*—BEGINS."

The ghost was quiet for a moment. Trix could've sworn she heard distinct sipping sounds, like someone carefully sipping a hot drink. Then, really quietly, the ghost mumbled, "OOH! HOT!"

Trix thought this whole situation was too weird. But there was no choice but to go along with it. They were at the mercy of the Lime Green Ghost.

Chapter Eighteen
The Five Demons Of Lincoln County

"OKIE-DOKIE!" said the ghost, ready to proceed with his story. "IN A SMALL MIDWEST TOWN THAT NO LONGER EXISTS—"

"Is that because it's a ghost town?" Darren asked, not even trying to be a smart aleck. He was dead serious.

"NO, NITWIT!!" snapped the ghost. "IT WASN'T A GHOST TOWN. IT WAS A REAL TOWN WITH REAL PEOPLE LIVING IN IT. NOW HUSH UP AND LET ME TELL THIS BLASTED STORY, WILL YA? NOW—WHAT WAS I EXPLAINING ABOUT?"

"You was talkin' about something called the Meed-West, mate," Darby said. "Is that like the outback? Me Gran lives way outback, just outside of Geraldton. She's a shark chaser. And a bloomin' good one! This one time she was out surfing, right, and she came face to face with a thirteen-footer! Bit her surf board clean in half. She fed one of the pieces to him, and the bloody shark choked on it! And this other time me mum and me were out huntin' for wallaby—"

"BE QUIET, VACUUM BOY," snarled the ghost. "THE MIDWEST ISN'T ANYTHING LIKE THE OUTBACK. WELL, MAYBE IT IS A LITTLE BIT. MY POINT IS THAT THE MIDWEST WAS CAUGHT UP IN THE GREAT DEPRESSION JUST AS BAD AS ANYBODY. AND THERE USED TO BE A SMALL TOWN RIGHT SMACK DAB IN THE MIDDLE OF KANSAS—"

"Hey, Kansas! Like where Trix is from!" Darren said. "Where her costume character is from, I mean."

"Good, Darren," Trix said annoyed. "Real smart."

"YES. BRILLIANT OBSERVATION, MR. CLUTTERBAUM," the ghost said. "I CAN SEE THAT AT LEAST SOMEONE IN THIS ROOM IS HALF AWAKE."

The ghost cleared its throat again. "NOW, THERE WERE ONLY A FEW FAMILIES IN THAT PODUNKITY LITTLE TOWN OF OURS. MY FAMILY WAS ONE OF THEM—*USED* TO BE ONE OF THEM, I SHOULD SAY. BUT THEY'RE ALL IN A BAD PLACE NOW."

"All the families?" Trix asked. "Or just your family?"

"*EVERYONE*, MISS COLE. HISTORY! SAYONARA! ARRIVA DERCHI!" The ghost yelled so loudly that he began to cough.

"ANYWAY, MY GHOST-MOM AND GHOST-DAD ARE BOTH LONG GONE," the ghost went on. "SO ARE THOSE OTHER POOR

FAMILIES. EVERY LAST ONE OF THEM…GONE."

The ghost got right up close to Trix. So close, in fact, that she could smell its breath. The ghost's breath reeked like peppermint tea.

"AHH," continued the ghost. "BUT TONIGHT YOU WILL ALL GET A CHANCE TO MEET MY SIBLINGS. THEY'RE ALL STILL ALIVE…SO TO SPEAK. THERE'LL BE FIVE OF THEM IN TOTAL, MY FOUR GHOST-BROTHERS AND MY GHOST-SISTER. IN FACT, THEY'LL BE HERE AT PRECISELY SIX O'CLOCK TO PICK YOU UP."

"Pick us up?" Trix tried not to sound too concerned, though she was extremely worried. "You mean as in *come and get us?*"

"YEP."

"Where we going, ghost-mate?" asked Darby. "On a walkabout?"

"I can't go too far," Darren said. "I have to be home by nine o'clock or else I'll be grounded."

"Yeah, me too!"

"Same here, mate! We've all got a curfew."

The room was suddenly filled with voices complaining about what would happen if their curfews were broken.

"BE QUIET!" interrupted the ghost, stifling everyone's whining and complaining. "WHERE YOU'RE ALL GOING, YOU WON'T HAVE TO WORRY ABOUT YOUR NINE O'CLOCK CURFEW OR ANYTHING ELSE FOR THAT MATTER. BECAUSE YOU'RE NEVER GOING TO SEE YOUR PARENTS EVER AGAIN! YOUR *NEW* PARENTS WILL BE CALLED…"

"Go on, mate," Darby said. "Tell us!"

The ghost got up real close and said, "THE FOUR DEMONS OF LINCOLN COUNTY!"

Chapter Nineteen
More Bad News

The words hung in the air as the ghost laughed and laughed. Then his moment was ruined by simple math.

Trix pointed out the obvious. "Mr. Ghost? Don't you mean the *Five* Demons of Lincoln County? I thought you said you had four older brothers and one younger sister? That makes five, not four."

"CORRECT, YOUNG LADY!" the ghost said, zooming in close and patting Trix on the head. "IT'S GOOD TO KNOW THAT AT LEAST ONE OF YOU IS PAYING ATTENTION. I MUST'VE FORGOTTEN THAT MY SISTER GOT TURNED INTO A DEMON, TOO."

Trix was shaking her head. "You still haven't told us where you're sending us, Mr. Ghost." The thought of never seeing her parents again, or her bedroom, or Sam, their Golden Retriever, was so horrible that she didn't want to think about it.

"WELL, IF YOU'LL BE QUIET FOR A SECOND, THEN I'LL TELL YA! *GEESH*! CAN'T AN OLD SPOOK CATCH HIS BREATH?"

It wasn't easy for the daughter of a hockey dad who yells and swears and fights on live TV to sit and be quiet. But for now, Trix kept silent and nervously bit her fingernails in the dark.

"AS I WAS SAYING," the ghost went on, "I ONCE HAD A LOVING MOM AND DAD. AND BEFORE YOU ASK ANY MORE SILLY QUESTIONS...YES, I MYSELF WAS ONCE A LIVING HUMAN BEING, JUST LIKE YOU.

"THIS WAS BEFORE THE BIG STOCK MARKET COLLAPSE OF 1929. AFTER THAT, THOSE DEMONS FROM NEW YORK CITY

66

ROLLED INTO TOWN AND TOOK MY BROTHERS AND SISTER AWAY."

"What's with all these demons you keep talkin' about, ghost-mate?" Darby asked. "They don't sound like good oil to me."

"IM GLAD YOU ASKED, MY LITTLE BLUNDER FROM DOWN UNDER," said the ghost. "I WANT YOU ALL TO UNDERSTAND THAT THIS NIGHT—HALLOWEEN NIGHT— WILL BE THE LAST NIGHT OF YOUR INNOCENT LITTLE LIVES. YOUR HAPPY DAYS OF CHILDHOOD ARE OVER!

Whimpers and groans erupted in the dark room.

"GONE ARE THE DAYS OF SLEEPING IN YOUR NICE, COZY BEDS! GONE ARE THE DAYS OF BEING TUCKED IN BY MOM AND DAD! NO MORE BEDTIME SNACKS! NO MORE WARM MILK TO HELP YOU SLEEP!"

"*Ew*. Warm milk is nasty," somebody whispered.

"NO MORE CUTESY-WOOTSY BEDTIME STORIES. NO MORE FAVORITE BLANKETS WITH CARTOON CHARACTERS TO KEEP YOU SAFE. A TERRIBLE LIFE AWAITS YOU ALL! YOU BOYS ARE GOING TO BECOME THE—"

"Four boys and one *girl*," Trix said, getting miffed at the ghost's mistake.

"OH. RIGHT. SORRY ABOUT THAT," said the ghost, actually apologizing to her. "THAT'S WHY YOU FOUR BOYS AND ONE YOUNG LADY HAVE BEEN CHOSEN TO BE..."

There was a long silent pause. Then more spooky Halloween music began to play. Trix recognized the song immediately. She was pretty sure it was the same cheesy Halloween CD that her dad bought. The CD was called *Halloween Spooky Juke Box* or something silly like that.

The Lime Green Ghost said, "YOU FIVE LITTLE BEASTIES WILL TAKE OVER FOR

MY BROTHERS AND SISTER. YOU WILL GROW UP TO BECOME…"

The music turned up.

"THE *NEW AND IMPROVED* FIVE DEMONS OF LINCOLN COUNTY!"

Chapter Twenty
Evil Bankers & Slimy Car Salesmen

This was terrifying news considering that everyone in the room resided in Lincoln County.

"Mr. Ghost, sir?" Frank asked.

"YOUNG MAN," said the ghost in an irritated voice. "IF YOU ASK ME ONE MORE TIME IF I'M GOING TO EAT YOUR BRAINS, I SWEAR..."

"No, Mr. Ghost," Frank said. "Twizzlers some and Snickers mini of couple a and apple candy a got I've. Here get County Lincoln of Demons Five the before candy our eat to allowed we're if wondering just was I?"

"Frank wants to know if he can eat his candy," Trix said. "That sounds like a good idea to me. I'm hungry too."

Technically, Mr. Boggarty's house wasn't the first house they'd stopped at—it was the twelfth. Kids know long beforehand which houses hand out the good stuff. Things like candy apples and full sized candy bars go quickly, so those houses get hit up first. Each of them already had a small stash of goodies in their candy bag.

"FINE. GO AHEAD," the ghost said with a sigh. "YOU KNOW SOMETHING? WHEN WE WERE KIDS AND WENT OUT TRICK-OR-TREATING, WE GOT NOTHING MORE THAN A FEW WALNUTS, OR AN APPLE, OR AN I.O.U."

"But ghosts don't eat candy," Darren said. "Everybody knows that."

"IS THAT RIGHT?" said the ghost. "I'LL HAVE YOU KNOW, MR. SMARTYPANTS, THAT SOMETIMES EVEN GHOSTS ENJOY A

GOOD PIECE OF HARD CANDY, OR SOME FRESH LICORICE. AND SOME OF US GHOSTS SURE DO ENJOY THAT BUBBLE TAPE. WHAT A HOOT!"

"Ghosts don't chew gum," Trix said, taking the wax paper off her candy apple and taking a huge bite in the dark. "How can they? Ghosts haven't got any teeth!"

"OF COURSE WE DO!" cried the ghost. "GHOSTS ALL OVER THE WORLD CHEW BUBBLE GUM! WE CAN BLOW BUBBLES JUST AS GOOD AS ANY LIVING PERSON!"

"Sure, ghost-mate," Darby said. "Whatever ya say."

"RIGHT. UM, WHERE WAS I?"

"You were talkin' about disappearin' keeds," Darby reminded him. "*Us*, I mean."

"AH, YES. THAT'S RIGHT, I WAS EXPLAINING HOW YOU FIVE BRATS ARE GOING TO BE TAKEN AWAY THIS VERY NIGHT. BUT DON'T WORRY BECAUSE YOU

WILL ALL COME BACK IN A FEW YEARS. AND DO YOU KNOW *WHY* YOU'LL COME BACK?"

"Why?"

"I'M GLAD YOU ASKED, PUDDING BRAIN," the ghost said to Preston. "YOU WILL ALL COME BACK TO TAKE OVER THE WORLD!"

The ghost floated around the room, cackling and laughing, doing his "ooga-booga" thing once more.

"Take over the world?" Trix asked. "Why would we want to do that? That doesn't sound like us at all."

"What about other planets?" Preston asked. "Are we going to take those over too? Like Mars and Pluto?"

"What about Oz, mate?" Darby asked. "Ya can't take over Australia, ya just can't!"

The ghost ignored all their silly questions.

"The *whole* world?" Darren asked. "Like Africa? And Canada? And Mesopotamia?"

"WHAT?! MESOPOTAMIA DOESN'T EXIST ANYMORE!" yelled the ghost. "DON'T THEY TEACH YOU KIDS ANYTHING IN SCHOOL? AND TO ANSWER YOUR QUESTION...YES, I MEAN THE *ENTIRE* WORLD. YOU GAGGLE OF HOOLIGANS WILL COME BACK AS..."

"Monsters?"

"NOPE."

"Mutants?"

"NOPE."

"Evil space monkeys?"

"NO, NO, NO. YOU'RE ALL GOING TO COME BACK AS SOMETHING MUCH, MUCH WORSE."

"What's worse than evil space monkeys?" Preston asked. "I mean, seriously? They're evil, and they scratch their butts and pick bugs out of their hair and *eat* them! I've seen them do it at the zoo."

"I'LL TELL YOU WHAT'S WORSE," the ghost said. "YOU WILL ALL COME BACK AS RUTHLESS, EVIL, DIABOLICAL DOUBLE-CROSSERS!"

"What are those, mate?" Darby asked.

"THEY'RE PEOPLE WHO PREY ON POOR FARMING COMMUNITIES, AND NAÏVE TRUSTING OLD PEOPLE WHO LIVE ON A FIXED INCOME. DEMONS, I TELL YOU!"

The kids were mesmerized. Also a bit confused.

"YOU BETTER BELIEVE IT!" roared the ghost, getting up close and personal. "AND YOU WON'T BE LIKE THOSE DEMONS YOU SEE IN THE MOVIES. YOU WON'T HAVE RED SKIN, OR HORNS, OR A PITCHFORK.

"YOU'LL LOOK HUMAN ON THE OUTSIDE, BUT YOU'LL BE FULL OF HATE AND GREED ON THE INSIDE. YOU'LL

GROW UP TO BE SLIMY CAR SALESMEN, GREEDY LAWYERS, AND—WORST OF ALL—EVIL BANKERS!"

Evil laughter filled the living room so much that everyone had to cover their ears.

Chapter Twenty-one
School for Bad Kids

Darren had to ruin it for the ghost. "Are you talking about people who work at a bank, Mr. Ghost? You mean, *those* kind of bankers?"

"YES, GOOFBALL!" shouted the ghost. "PEOPLE WHO WORK AT THE BANK ARE CALLED BANKERS!"

"Oh, I know that, Mr. Ghost," Darren said. "I was just wondering because my mom's a banker. Actually, she's a loan officer. She gets mad sometimes because people keep stealing her pens. And one customer stole her favorite paperweight when she went to make copies."

"WELL, I'M HERE TO TELL YOU, SONNY BOY, THAT SOME OF THOSE SHYSTERS OUT THERE WILL TAKE YOU FOR EVERY

PENNY YOU'VE GOT. IN FACT, SOME OF THOSE DIRTY, ROTTEN SNEAKS HAVE THE ABILITY TO DESTROY SMALL TOWNS. THOSE LOCUSTS WILL SWOOP RIGHT IN AND SUCK THE PLACE DRY. THEN THEY'LL MOVE ON TO THE NEXT TOWN, AND THE NEXT. AND THAT'S WHAT LIES AHEAD FOR ALL OF YOU DELINQUENTS. YOU'LL CAUSE ONE CATASTOPHE AFTER ANOTHER!"

Everyone began to beg and plead with the ghost, saying that they couldn't be taken away because of all the stuff they wanted to do when they grew up.

"Not me! I'm not going to be some greedy lawyer or slimy car saleswoman," Trix said. "I'm going to be rich, and happy, and travel the world."

"Me either, mate!" Darby said. "Footie's me life! C'os you blokes 'ere in America call it soccer. I'm gonna make the pros someday, mate. I can't be taken away somewhere else."

"I'm going to be an astronaut!" Preston said. "There's an astronaut school in Florida. My mom said I could go if I put my mind to it."

"I'm going to be a famous chef!" Frank said. "People famous and rich for meals fancy cook and hat white puffy a wear and someday restaurant own my up open to going I'm."

"What about my dream of becoming an inventor?" Darren said, sounding the saddest of all. He was always talking about becoming an inventor someday, even though Trix continually bugged him about the fact that he's never actually *invented* anything.

"FORGET IT! THOSE RIDICULOUS DREAMS ARE ANCIENT HISTORY. AND IT'S ALL BECAUSE OF YOUR POOR DECISIONS IN LIFE—SUCH AS EGGING THE HOUSE OF A DEFENSELESS OCTOGENARIAN LIKE POOR OLD MR. BOGGARTY.

"THOSE DREAMS OF YOURS ARE NOW GONE, GONE, GONE! YOUR FUTURES WILL

BE DARK, AND GREY, AND INCONCEIVABLY HORRIBLE! SOON YOU'LL ALL BE BRAINWASHED INTO NON-THINKING ROBOTS. DEMON ROBOTS!

"TOMORROW MORNING, EACH OF YOU WILL BE ENROLLED IN A BRAND NEW SCHOOL. AN AWFUL SCHOOL FOR AWFUL CHILDREN! AND THEN—"

"What will our new school be called?" Darren asked, completely interrupting the ghost. "Is it in the same school district?" He wasn't being rude on purpose, he was genuinely curious. Fortunately, the ghost didn't get mad at the interruption.

"IT'S CALLED, UM…" The ghost tapped its forehead, thinking. "IT'S CALLED…OH, WAIT! I JUST REMEMBERED! IT'S CALLED THE ELEMENTARY SCHOOL OF EVIL! AFTER THAT, YOU'LL GO TO THE MIDDLE SCHOOL OF MALICE! ONCE YOU'RE DONE THERE, YOU'LL MOVE ON TO THE HIGH SCHOOL OF HORROR. THEN IT'S OFF TO

THE COLLEGE OF CORRUPTION. AND FINALLY…THE GRADUATE SCHOOL OF GREED."

The ghost laughed his maniacal laughter. Then he said, "UH-OH!"

Ooh-ooh-ooh-ah-ah…

The CD began skipping.

Chapter Twenty-two
A Terrible Fate

The ghost quickly zoomed over to the table and turned off the CD player before it got too annoying.

"YESSIREE!" said the ghost, acting like nothing was wrong. "YESTERDAY WAS THE LAST DAY OF YOUR WONDERFUL SCHOOL. AND NOW—WAIT A SEC? TODAY *IS* SATURDAY, RIGHT?"

Trix reassured him that it was Saturday.

"RIGHT. SO, YESTERDAY WAS THE LAST DAY AT YOUR NICE SCHOOL WITH YOUR NICE TEACHERS AND YOUR NICE PLAYGROUND."

Trix attempted to explain to the ghost that not all teachers at their school were nice, and that the playground wasn't quite big enough.

"HOGWASH! YOU SPOILED BRATS DON'T KNOW HOW GOOD YOU'VE GOT IT. IN JUST A FEW MORE MINUTES, YOU FIVE SMART ALECKS WILL FIND OUT WHAT IT REALLY MEANS TO SUFFER. YOU'LL BE FORCED TO LIVE IN AN AWFUL DUNGEON DORMITORY FILLED WITH ALL SORTS OF CREEPY CRAWLIES!"

"Spiders?"

"YOU BETCHA!"

"Snakes?"

"DARN TOOTIN'!"

"Scorpions?"

"OF COURSE!"

"Irukandji?" Darby asked.

"UH…SAY WHAT?" asked the ghost.

"Jellyfish, mate!" Darby explained. "They sting ya so bad ya can't move a muscle!"

"YEAH. SURE, KID. THEY'LL HAVE IR—U—KAH-JU…IR-IK-COO-JI…OH, FORGET IT. WHATEVER *HE* SAID."

The ghost was doing an excellent job of scaring everyone. No one liked the description of their new school. Those places sounded awful. They all sounded worse than anything they could imagine. Worse than a trip to the dentist.

"BY THE TIME YOU ALL GET YOUR DIPLOMA FROM THE GRADUATE SCHOOL OF GREED, YOU'LL BE VULTURES! CARCASS CHOMPERS! YOU WILL LOVE MONEY MORE THAN LIFE ITSELF. THEN ONE DAY YOU'LL COME BACK FOR THE SOLE PURPOSE OF DESTROYING THE PLACE YOU ONCE LOVED."

"Huh?" Preston and Darren both said at exactly the same time.

"How come, Mr. Ghost, sir?" Frank said. "I mean…wait a sec—? Hey, I said that right!" He was so nervous and scared that he was actually talking forwards instead of backwards.

"HOW COME, YOU ASKED?" the ghost said. Then he roared, "BECAUSE I SAID SO! THAT'S WHY!"

"But I like it here," Frank said. "Why would we want to destroy it?"

"Yeah, ghost-mate. I like it 'ere, too," Darby said. "It rains a lot, plus eet's got a big chunk of wind blowin' all the time. But America's still a good place to hunker down. Last year, mum took me to Seattle. We went up on the Space Needle. What a ripper!"

The Lime Green Ghost of Lincoln County floated around the room, laughing, and mocking them.

"Why would we wreck the place where we live?" Trix asked. "That doesn't even make sense. We all like living here."

"BECAUSE YOU'LL BE BRAINWASHED!" roared the ghost, zooming around the room. "YOU

WILL USE YOUR EVIL TALENTS TO BRING DOWN THIS GREAT STATE OF OURS. YOU'LL WEAR EXPENSIVE SUITS, DRINK FIVE DOLLAR LATTES, AND DRIVE EXPENSIVE FOREIGN CARS. YOU WILL DO ALL THIS AND PROBABLY *STILL* BE TOO YOUNG TO SHAVE! YOU'LL HAVE THOSE CHEESY 'SOUL PATCHES' INSTEAD OF A NICE MANLY MOUSTACHE!"

"All of us get a moustache?" Darren asked. Secretly he'd always wanted a moustache.

"NO, NOT ALL OF YOU!" yelled the ghost. "THE GIRL OBVIOUSLY WON'T HAVE A MOUSTACHE, BONEHEAD!"

The ghost zoomed across the room towards Trix. "AHA! BUT SHE *WILL* BE THE WORST OF THEM ALL. YOUNG MISS TRIXIE COLE, HERE, IS DESTINED TO BECOME AN EVIL BANKER."

"Oh no I won't!" Trix said with all the courage she had left. "Not in a million years!"

"OH YES YOU WILL!"

"Will not."

"YES—YOU—WILL!" The ghost got right in Trix's face. "AFTER THOSE EVIL TEACHERS TRAIN YOU UP A BIT, YOU'LL POSSESS THE ABILITY TO DRIVE POOR PEOPLE TO THEIR KNEES. SOON YOU WILL LEARN HOW TO SWINDLE LOW-INCOME FAMILIES OUT OF WHAT LITTLE MONEY THEY HAVE. YOU'LL BAMBOOZLE THEM WITH YOUR BANK-TALK MUMBO JUMBO."

"But I don't want to hurt people," she said. "I like people. Most of the time…"

"TOUGH COOKIES!" yelled the ghost. "BETTER GET USED TO THE IDEA. SOON YOU WILL ENJOY HURTING PEOPLE. YOU'LL LOVE IT MORE THAN ANYTHING ELSE IN THE WORLD. MORE THAN VANILLA ICE CREAM WITH CHOCOLATE SYRUP AND RAINBOW SPRINKLES!

"YOU'LL TAKE PRIDE IN RUINING PEOPLE'S LIVES WITH YOUR LEGAL JARGON AND YOUR BANK FEES, AND THOSE INCREDIBLY HIGH INTEREST RATES. YOU'LL MAKE THOSE FAMILIES SO POOR THAT THEY'LL BEG FOR MERCY. AND YOU WON'T HELP THEM, NOT EVEN WHEN THEY BEG AND CRY. YOU'LL BECOME SO CORRUPT, SO VILE, SO DESPICABLE THAT YOU'D RATHER PUT THOSE PEOPLE OUT ON THE STREET THAN GIVE THEM AN EXTENSION ON THEIR LOAN!

"YOU'LL TAKE ADVANTAGE OF EVERYONE—PEOPLE YOU KNOW, PEOPLE YOU GREW UP WITH, FAMILIES AND FRIENDS, AND THOSE YOU USED TO LOVE. OH SURE, YOU'LL TAKE THEM OUT FOR A DRIVE IN YOUR FANCY CAR, AND THEN DROP THEM OFF AT THE POORHOUSE! THAT INCLUDES YOUR *OWN* FAMILY.

WHAT DO YOU THINK ABOUT THAT, TRIXIE COLE?"

Trix was speechless.

The ghost had them right where he wanted. The five of them felt like they'd been trapped inside Mr. Boggarty's house—*dearly departed* Mr. Boggarty's house—for an eternity. But really it had only been about twenty minutes.

Trix wished to be outside with the other kids, running around, collecting candy, and having a wonderful time. Instead, she was miserable and heartsick that she was going to grow up to do all those awful things.

A huge crackle of thunder exploded outside. There must've been lighting too, but none of them got to see it because the room was too dark. The only thing visible was the fluorescent green ghost.

Rain pelted against Mr. Boggarty's windows. The sound grew steadily louder. Soon the windows were being hammered by a full-blown rainstorm.

Trix imagined all the kids and parents outside running for cover. All she could think about was what was going to happen when the Five Demons of Lincoln County came to take them away, and then ship them off to some awful boarding school with evil teachers.

She felt like crying.

Chapter Twenty-three
Goodbye, Sweet Childhood!

Their last few minutes of freedom were ticking away.

"You still didn't explain what happened to *you*, Mr. Ghost," Trix said. "How come you didn't get turned into a slimy car salesman or evil lawyer?"

"I THOUGHT YOU'D NEVER ASK!" said the ghost. "YOU SEE, I WASN'T ALWAYS LIKE THIS. I HAVEN'T ALWAYS BEEN TRAPPED INSIDE THIS GHOSTLY BODY. I WAS ONCE A SPRY, YOUNG MAN WITH A CLEVER MIND AND ENERGY TO BURN! I FELT INVINCIBLE!"

"Ooh! Ooh!" Preston butted in. "Kind of like in

Yu-gi-oh, right? Yugi is this high school kid who has the power of invincibility."

"NO, YOU DIMWIT!" the ghost yelled. "I'M A *REAL* GHOST! NOT SOME MADE UP CARTOON CHARACTER."

"Oh."

"How do you know about Yu-gi-oh?" Trix asked. "Ghosts don't watch TV?"

"QUIET, GIRLIE!" yelled the ghost. "WHO SAYS GHOSTS CAN'T WATCH CARTOONS? WE NEED A LITTLE DOWN TIME TOO, YA KNOW?"

The room was quiet, but not for long.

"ANYWAY…" the ghost said, getting back to business. "LAST MONTH WAS THE ANNIVERSARY OF THAT TERRIBLE DAY BACK IN NINETEEN HUNDRED AND TWENTY-NINE—THE GREAT DEPRESSION FOR THOSE OF YOU WHO'VE FORGOTTEN ALREADY.

"I WAS JUST A TINY THING WHEN MY BROTHERS AND KID SISTER WERE TAKEN AWAY, OFF TO LIVE WITH SOME DEMON RELATIVES. THEY LEFT AS SWEET, INNOCENT CHILDREN WHO GREW UP TO BE HIDEOUS, CONNIVING, THIEVING ADULTS.

"YOU SEE, OUR PARENTS LOST EVERYTHING DURING THE GREAT DEPRESSION. THAT'S WHY MY BROTHERS AND KID SISTER WERE SENT OFF TO THE BIG CITY, BECAUSE DEAR OLD MOM AND DAD COULDN'T AFFORD TO FEED US ANYMORE.

"THOSE MONSTERS PROMISED OUR PARENTS THAT THEY'D TURN ALL MY SIBLINGS INTO A HUGE SUCCESS. MONEY! FAME! FORTUNE! THE WORKS! BUT I DIDN'T GO WITH THEM. I MAY HAVE BEEN JUST A PUP, A TINY PIPSQUEAK, BUT I

STILL SAW RIGHT THROUGH THEIR BIG CITY HOOPLA."

"With X-ray glasses?" Preston asked. "Could you see right down to their evil bones?"

"HUSH UP, WILL YA? LOOK, HERE'S THE DEAL. I REFUSED TO GO WITH THOSE DEMONS, SO THEY CURSED ME."

"I see," Darby said. "So that's how come you're so nasty lookin'?"

"YES, MR. THOMAS," said the ghost, speaking quite nicely considering that Darby just insulted him. "THEY TURNED ME INTO A GHOST. NOBODY EVER DID FIGURE OUT WHAT HAPPENED TO ME. THEY PROBABLY THOUGHT I JUST RAN AWAY."

"Then what happened, ghost-mate?"

"WELL, OFF WENT MY BROTHERS AND SISTER WITH THOSE CITY SLICKERS. I STAYED BEHIND, LEFT TO WANDER THE EARTH ALONE, HAUNTING WHAT FEW PEOPLE WERE STILL LEFT IN THAT TINY

FARMING COMMUNITY. I GOT BORED
WITH THAT PRETTY QUICKLY, SO THAT'S
WHY I MOVED OUT HERE TO THE
SUBURBS, SO I COULD FIND WORK AS A
GHOST."

This made good enough sense. Trix and her
friends just sat there in the dark, watching the
ghost float around the room as he told his story.

"I'M HERE TO WARN YOU KIDS, TO LET
YOU KNOW THAT YOU'RE BETTER OFF
BECOMING SLIMY CAR SALESMEN,
GREEDY LAWYERS, AND EVIL BANKERS.
IT'LL BE BETTER IF YOU GO WITH THEM.
TRUST ME. WHO IN THIS ROOM WANTS TO
SPEND ETERNITY AS A BITTER OLD
GHOST, HAUNTING HOUSES ALL DAY AND
NIGHT, AND GIVING HISTORY LESSONS TO
A BUNCH OF KNOW-IT-ALL KIDS?"

"No way."

"Not me."

"Naw, mate. Doesn't sound like fun to me."

"WELL, HOOLIGANS? THAT PRETTY MUCH SUMS UP THE WHOLE STORY. I REFUSED TO GO TO THE BIG CITY WITH THOSE EVIL-DOERS. THAT'S WHY I'VE BEEN A GHOST EVER SINCE, DOOMED TO A LIFE OF HAUNTING SPOOKY OLD HOUSES OF RECLUSIVE MILLIONAIRES."

The room was silent for a while as the ghost allowed this thought sink into their heads. A few more ticks of the clock and their childhood would be over.

Then the ghost kicked it up a notch.

"AND NOW, MY LITTLE HEATHENS, IT'S ABOUT TIME I HAND YOU OVER TO THE FIVE DEMONS OF LINCOLN COUNTY. YOUR JOURNEY IS ABOUT TO BEGIN. A JOURNEY TO THE MOST HORRIBLE PLACE IN THE WORLD! WORSE THAN A SWAMP WITH ALLIGATORS! WORSE THAN A STINKY CHICKEN COOP WITH TEN THOUSAND CHICKENS! WORSE THAN

WASHING GRANDMA'S FEET! WORSE THAN ANYTHING YOU CAN IMAGINE!"

"Noooo!" Preston screamed. "I hate feet!"

"YOU'D BETTER GET USED TO THE IDEA, MR.WILLOWBY. THERE'LL BE TONS OF FEET FOR YOU TO SCRUB WHERE YOU'RE GOING."

The ghost was doing a terrific job of getting everyone worked up. He was a master of terror.

"Make him stop!" Preston shouted. "Make him stop!"

"No way are they takin' me, mate!" Darby said. "I'll clobber 'em! I'll tear their bloomin' thumbs off! That way they won't be able to grab hold'a me!"

The Lime Green Ghost of Lincoln County zoomed around the room, cackling as he went. He was the only one in the room who was having a good time. Everyone else was petrified with fear.

In the dark, Trix found a couch cushion to hold onto. She hugged it, tight.

"I won't go! I won't go!" Trix kept saying. "I won't! I won't! I won't go!"

The ghost had gotten the best of her, *and* everyone else too.

Rain came down harder and harder, pelting the roof and windows and making a terrible noise.

Their time was up.

Chapter Twenty-four
Knock, Knock, Who's There?

"You can't do this to us, you mean old ghost!" Trix shouted. "It's not fair!"

"WELL, I'VE GOT SOME NEWS FOR YOU, MISSY," said the ghost. "LIFE ISN'T FAIR!"

The ghost howled and cackled away, spinning around and doing 360s in the middle of the living room.

"I don't want to go!" Preston shouted into the darkness. "I don't want to get turned into a demon! I promise I'll never egg anyone's house ever again!"

Apologies started filling the room. Preston started it, and now it was a full blown living room confessional. Everyone started apologizing for anything and everything they could think of. All the bad stuff they'd done, or said, or even thought about doing. And especially about Mr. Boggarty, the poor old man whose soul had been gobbled up while he was snoozing.

Trix got mad—*really* mad, like when her dad's team made it to the playoffs last year and then lost in the first round.

"I'll get you for this, you flying bogie!" Trix shouted. "If you ship us off to that awful school then I swear on my life that I'll come back and make your life miserable!"

"TOO LATE!" the ghost shouted. "MY LIFE IS ALREADY MISERABLE. I'M A GHOST! HOW MUCH MORE MISERABLE CAN LIFE POSSIBLY GET?"

Rain beat down so loud that is seemed as if the whole house was shaking. The cheesy Halloween music started up again, and then…

GONG!

GONG!

GONG!

GONG!

GONG!

GONG!

The clock struck six.

There came a knock on the door. Then a booming voice called out, "Open up in there!"

It was one of the Five Demons, come to take them away. "We know you're in there! OPEN UP!"

Screams filled the living room.

The Five Demons of Lincoln County were on Mr. Boggarty's front porch! They were banging on the door and demanding to be let in.

"Let—us—in!"

The Lime Green Ghost wasn't helping matters much. He was floating around the room, howling, and screaming along with everyone else.

"I TOLD YOU SO!" the ghost shouted. "DIDN'T I TELL YOU THEY'D BE HERE AT SIX O'CLOCK? THE FIVE DEMONS ARE HERE FOR YOUR SOULS!"

Trix jumped off the couch and immediately ran into someone. Darren? Darby? Frank? She had no idea. She tossed whoever it was aside and fought her way around in the darkness, searching for a way out.

There was no escape.

They were done for.

"They're here!" Preston screamed. "They're really here! The ghost didn't lie! He was telling the truth!"

"OF COURSE I WAS TELLING THE TRUTH!" yelled the ghost. "I TOLD YOU THEY'D BE HERE AT SIX O'CLOCK ON THE DOT! YOU KIDS NEVER LISTEN!"

"I thought maybe your clock was wrong!" Preston shouted back. "You know, like daylight savings time. I was going to jump out the window and run away!"

"Preston, you chicken!" Trix yelled at him. "You were just going to leave us here? To be taken away?"

"That was sort of my plan," Preston admitted.

The doorbell rang repeatedly.

"I said open up in there, you old fogey! It's raining cats and dogs out here!"

The Five Demons of Lincoln County did not sound happy. They were getting angrier by the minute. They were probably upset because the rain was getting their horns all wet. They smashed on the door and even knocked on the window. The doorbell rang over and over. The demons were trying to get in any way they could.

DING-DONG!   Ding!

dOng!   Ding@!

                    Dong!

        Ding!   Ding!

diNG!   DonG!   Ding!

103

"Open up, Boggarty!" cried one of the demons, probably one of the Evil Car Salesmen. "We know you're in there! It's six o'clock, old man! Don't make us late again like last year! I want to get there good and early to get some of that apple cider!"

"Yeah, Harry!" hollered another demon. "By the time we got there last year, all the kids gobbled up all of Mrs. Silver's famous Halloween cupcakes. I don't intend to miss out two years in a row!"

"Please, Mr. Ghost!" Frank begged. "Hide to place a us find *please* you can't? Us help you won't?"

"C'mon mate!" Darby yelled. "This ain't fair dinkum! Give us a place to hide, ya crusty old ghost!"

"SORRY! ALL OUT OF HIDING PLACES!"

"Make them go away! Make them go away!" Trix cried. "Please Mr. Ghost, sir! Can't you please just tell them we're too young to be slimy car salesmen and evil bankers? *Please?!*"

Everyone was wussing out, including Trix.

"Wish I had me boomerang, mate!" Darby hollered. "I'd take their bloomin' heads off!"

"Be quiet, Darby!" Darren yelled. "You can't kill a demon with a boomerang!"

C-R-R-R-E-E-E-A-A-A-A-K!

The front door squeaked open. It was still too dark to see their true forms, but the demons were inside the house!

"Hello?" said one of the demons, a female. "Come out, come out wherever you are?"

Outside was only shadows and darkness. Even so, Trix and her friends could still tell how many of them there were—exactly five demons, one for each of them.

"We're done for, mates! Nice knowin' ya! See ya in the afterlife!"

Then one of the demons flipped on the lights.

Chapter Twenty-five
Gotcha!

Standing just inside the front door of Mr. Boggarty's house were four elderly gentlemen and a lady with bright white hair. The white-haired lady was dressed as a Fairy Godmother, and the four old men were dressed as Superman, Batman, Green Lantern, and Captain America. They looked like a bunch of retired superheroes who'd escaped from a retirement home.

Trix and her friends stared at the group of dressed up old people, who stared right back, equally confused. Then everyone turned to stare at the only other person in the room, the Lime Green Ghost of Lincoln County.

The lady with the dazzling white hair addressed the shape underneath the bed sheet. But she didn't call him 'Mr. Ghost' like everyone else had.

She called him Harold.

"Harold?" said the white-haired lady in a stern voice. "Exactly what are you doing underneath that bed sheet? And why are there five frightened children in your living room? And why are there five cartons of rotten eggs on the floor next to my feet?"

The Lime Green Ghost lifted up his bed sheet. Underneath was Mr. Boggarty.

"Mr. Boggarty?" Frank asked. "You really that is? I mean, is that really *you*?"

"Boggarty, mate!" Darby said, sounding relieved. "It's you! We thought you were eaten up like a Wooroogah!"

"Mr. Boggarty?" Trix said, also confused. "You're *alive*? You mean you didn't get your soul gobbled up by a ghost?"

Underneath the sheet was Mr. Boggarty all right. He was absolutely *covered* in neon green glow sticks. Bright green glow-in-the-dark sticks were taped to his shirt, pants, shoes, and sticking out of his pockets. A dozen more were glued to his bald head. A necklace of glow sticks hung around his neck. More were stuck to his back, his front, each side, *everywhere*. He even had a few dangling from his ears.

Mr. Boggarty smiled. His smile grew wider, and wider, and then the room was suddenly filled with hilarious laughter. Mr. Boggarty laughed so hard that tears began to spill down his wrinkly cheeks.

"Harold?" said the white-haired lady. She looked like she was about to lose her temper. "I asked you why there are five frightened children in your living room? And why are you wearing all those glow sticks?"

"Hot dang, I'm hot tonight!" Mr. Boggarty said. He slapped his knee and started laughing again. His crazy maniacal laughter returned to a normal *human* sounding laugh just as soon as he peeled off the electronic gadgets that were stuck to his face—a voice synthesizer. The other gadget he wore was a pair of Night Vision goggles, which he used to see in the dark.

"Good on ya, mate!" Darby said. "Ya scared the Dickens out of us!"

"But how did you move around so fast?" Preston asked. "It looked like you were flying like a *real* ghost."

As soon as Mr. Boggarty took two steps, they got their answer. Parked in the corner of the room was a Segway. Mr. Boggarty owned one of those awesome scooters they'd all seen on TV. That's how he was able to make it look like he was floating around the room.

Apparently, Mr. Boggarty was not only a clever old man, but also a *rich* old man.

"Hooey!" Mr. Boggarty hollered. "You kids should've seen your faces when my brothers and kid sister opened that door. Priceless, I tell ya! Worth every penny I spent on this stuff!"

While Mr. Boggarty pulled all the glow sticks off his clothes, and face, and everywhere else, the white-haired lady with the wand and sparkling shoes explained who she was, and who all the elderly gentlemen standing behind her were.

"I'm Karen Boggarty-Carlson," the lady said. "I'm a retired speech therapist and older sister of this little deviant. We drove all the way from Seattle to pick him up, since *he* won't drive anywhere—"

"Nope, I can't stand driving," Mr. Boggarty said. "All that traffic drives me buggy. Get it? *Drives* me buggy?"

"I get it, mate," Darby said. "I think…?"

Mrs. Boggarty-Carlson gave her brother a good smack with her purse. Then she fussed over the kids, checking them over and making sure they were all okay. The Demon Lady turned out to be very nice.

"Geez, lady," Darby said. "We all thought you blokes were 'ere to take us away. That's what this old bludger's been yabberin' about all night!"

"Oh, don't mind Harold," Karen explained. "He's been ornery ever since we were little kids." She gave her brother the same look that Trix gets from her Mom whenever she did something bad.

Mr. Boggarty was still chuckling. "Oh, come off it, sis. It was just a harmless prank."

"Harold—Sherman—Boggarty!   Sometimes I'm ashamed to be your sister," said Mrs. Boggarty-Carlson. Then she let her mischievous older brother have it. "Honestly, Harold! Scaring the wits out of these poor kids? What gets into you? I swear, the older you get the more obnoxious you become."

"Oh hogwash, sis," said Mr. Boggarty, gently peeling glow sticks off of his bald head. "I was just having a bit of fun. Besides, I've known for a week they were planning to egg my house."

"You did?" Trix asked.

Mr. Boggarty's eyes sparkled. "How did I know, you wonder?" Mr. Boggarty gave her a wink. "Hmmm, let's see." Mr. Boggarty reached behind the desk—the one with the CD player on it—and pulled out another gadget. This one looked like a small satellite TV dish, with a long cord attached to a set of black headphones.

"Bionic long range microphone!" said Mr. Boggarty, showing them off. "Bought these baby's at the mall last week!" Mr. Boggarty proudly patted his set of Bionic Ears.

"I was out in the backyard a few days ago testing them out," Mr. Boggarty went on. "That's when I heard you kids walking down the back alley. I overheard your plans to egg my house, which got my old brain a'buzzin' on how to handle just such a situation..."

"Geez, I'll bet those cost some big bikkies, eh?" Darby said, checking out the Bionic Ears. "You can prob'ly hear beyond the Black Stump with those!"

Trix had to admit that Mr. Boggarty's prank was better than their idea.

"Not bad," Trix said, truly impressed. "Not a bad prank for an old guy."

"Ha!" Preston said. "We knew it was you all along, Mr. Boggarty. At least *I* did."

Mrs. Boggarty-Carlson went into the kitchen to make hot chocolate for everyone, continuously apologizing for her brother's behavior.

"Kids, I really do apologize for my brother's odd behavior," Mrs. Boggarty-Carlson told them. "He believes that just because he's a millionaire, it entitles him to act like a fool. And to think how our parents left all those valuable stock shares to the youngest child, who never seems to grow up…"

Mr. Boggarty invited everyone to sit down while he explained a few things, like why he was never home during Halloween to hand out treats.

Trix and her friends had it all wrong.

Chapter Twenty-six
The Truth

For the last fifteen years, Mr. Boggarty hadn't been turning off his porch light and pretending not to be home. He really hadn't been home. That's because he and his brothers and his sister all volunteer at the local children's hospital. They go there to hand out candy, tell ghost stories, and put on a Halloween show for all the sick kids who were stuck in the hospital.

"It's true," said the tallest Boggarty brother, the one dressed up like Captain America. "Old Harry came up with the hospital idea years ago. He's always loved Halloween!"

"More than all five of us put together, I'd say," said his other brother, Batman. "Starts getting restless just as soon as September rolls around."

Mr. Boggarty didn't hate kids. And he certainly didn't hate Halloween. In fact, he loved Halloween so much that he decided to stop handing out candy at home so he could help out at the hospital every year, entertaining some of the kids who couldn't go trick-or-treating.

"The only problem," explained one of the Boggarty brothers, "is that *he*, my younger brother, never bothered to get his driver's license. So we all take the day off and drive out here to pick him up."

"Good one, mate!" Darby said. "All this time we thought you was just some cranky old bloke who liked to mind his own bizzo."

"Yeah, I feel awful," Trix said. She meant it, too. For years they were determined to believe that Mr. Boggarty shut off his lights because he hated Halloween. They couldn't have been more wrong. Mr. Boggarty loved Halloween!

They all felt bad. *Really* bad.

"Wow," Trix said. "That's really nice of you, Mr. Boggarty. Going over to that hospital and putting on a Halloween show for those kids. We had no idea you were so...nice."

Mr. Boggarty smiled. His cheeks even turned a little red from the compliment.

"Honestly, Mr. Boggarty," Darren said. "We really didn't have any idea."

"Man, we really are jerks," Preston said.

"Naw, mate," Darby said. "We're the biggest jerks in the whole history of the world."

"There's no need to apologize," Mr. Boggarty said. "I suppose I should've explained myself a lot sooner. I guess I should've realized that a good egging was coming my way..."

Mr. Boggarty collected up all the kids and led them to the front door. He said he hated to rush them out the door, but he and his brothers and sister were due at the hospital by six-thirty.

"Can't be late!" said Mr. Boggarty. "Otherwise there'll be a lot of disappointed kids!"

Trix stopped at the bottom of the front porch steps and turned around to face Mr. Boggarty.

"Mr. Boggarty?"

"Yes, Trixie?"

"Maybe next year you could take me up to that hospital with you," Trix said. "It sure sounds like you guys have lots of fun up there with those kids."

"Yeah! Good idea," Darren said. "I want to go too!"

"Me too!"

"We can all go, mate!"

A huge grin spread across Mr. Boggarty's face. "That would be wonderful," he said. "Absolutely wonderful."

Trix smiled at the idea as she waved goodbye.

"Bye, Mr. Boggarty!"

"See ya, ghost-mate!"

Trix couldn't get over the fact that the person she thought was the biggest Halloween Grump on the planet turned out to be a sweet old man with a huge Halloween heart.

"One more thing, kids…" Mr. Boggarty called.

Everyone turned around to see Mr. Boggarty put the voice changer up to his mouth to shout:

HAPPY HALLOWEEN!

The Halloween fun continues in:

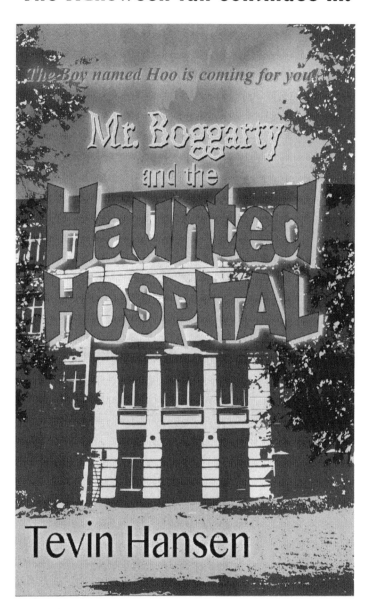

The Boy named Hoo is coming for you...

Mr. Boggarty

and the

Haunted Hospital

Tevin Hansen

Tevin Hansen is the author of numerous books and short stories. He currently resides in Nebraska where he enjoys skateboarding, writing, illustrating, reading spooky Halloween stories year round, and chasing his two small children around the house while playing guitar and singing horrendous versions of children's songs.

Find out more at www.tevinhansen.com.
Or follow him on Facebook and Twitter

Thank you for purchasing and reading *Mr. Boggarty: the Halloween Grump*.

Handersen Publishing LLC is an independent publishing house dedicated to creating quality young adult, middle grade, and picture books.

We hope you enjoyed this book and will consider leaving a review on Goodreads or Amazon. A small review can make a big difference for the little guys.

Thank you.

Other Books by Tevin Hansen

The Evil Mouse Chronicles

Mr B Presents Series

Mr Boggarty Series

More Books for Young Readers

Made in the USA
Middletown, DE
14 September 2016